To my son Tejinder Singh and my daughter Tejkiran Kaur, who are proud of their unique identity.

P.S.

Coloring Story Book

580 College Avenue, Palo Alto, California 94306, USA
Phone (650) 494-7454 **fax** (650) 494-3316
e-mail info@sikhfoundation.org **website** www.sikhfoundation.org
The Sikh Foundation is a non-profit, non-political organization, founded in 1967 that strives to preserve and promote Sikh heritage in the West.

OBJECTIVES
- Pass on the Sikh heritage to the growing Sikh Diaspora in the West, particularly the youth
- Introduce the world to the ethics, mysticism, arts, literature and heroism of the Sikhs
- Contribute Sikh perspectives to issues of common human concern
- Advance Sikh culture by advancing the tradition of critical and creative thinking that gave birth to the faith
- Generate the highest quality resources for the study of Sikhism

Our projects, sponsorships and collaborations include:
- Academic courses, conferences and chairs of Sikh studies at leading universities in the West
- Sikh art exhibitions and establishing permanent Sikh art galleries at major museums worldwide
- Renovation and conservation of historical Sikh monuments
- Provide the community with the highest quality printed materials on Sikhism such as books, journals, calendars, posters, displays, greeting cards and other Sikh pride building products

THE BOY WITH LONG HAIR
Approved as Supplemental Instructional Material for K – 3 grades by California Department of Education
First published in 1999.
2nd EDITION, 2003, DESIGN & PRODUCTION: inkfish, Los Angeles, California USA
3rd EDITION, 2012 DESIGN & PRODUCTION: United Graphics

The Boy With Long Hair

Colored by _____

(Your Name)

I wish I could go back to my old school.

At my old school, Mama dropped me off there. Sometimes we walked together,

and sometimes we went in the car,
both Mama and I.

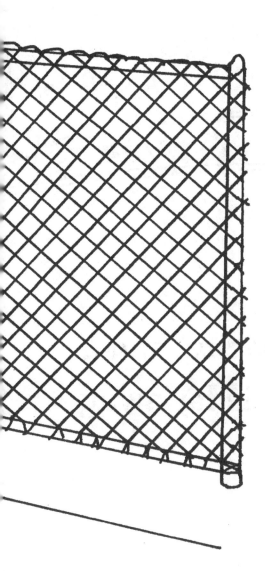

In my old school, I had many friends. Everyday we played together in the playground. I was happy.

Then we moved to a new city, and a new school. My new school is far away from home.

I have to ride the school bus.

Everyday, I stand alone at the bus stop. There are other children there but nobody talks to me. They all look at me in a strange way. So, I stand alone.

Sometimes, I look at the passing cars. Sometimes, I look at the birds flying by. And sometimes, I just draw circles with my shoe. I wish I didn't have to stand alone. May be they don't like me because I look different.

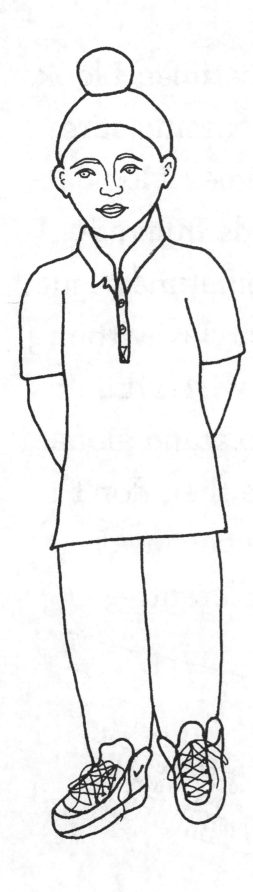

You see, I am the boy with long hair. I have long hair because I don't cut it. We are the Sikhs from India. The Sikhs are not supposed to cut their hair- ever, not even the boys. I like the way I look, with my long hair.

comb

joorda

patka

Every morning, I comb my hair
down and roll it up into a joorda.
Then I tie a Patka, a small cloth over
it to keep it neatly tied up.

When I grow up, I will have a beard and a mustache, and I will wear a turban, just like Daddy. I think Daddy looks cool.

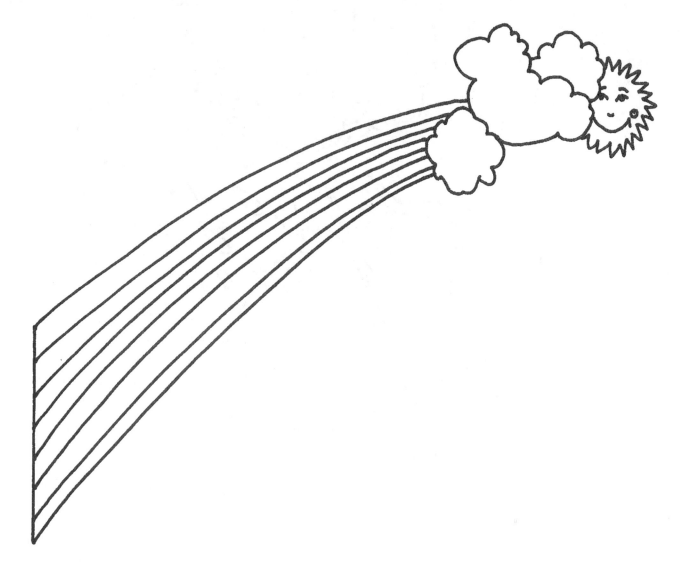

You see, although we all look different, we are also the same in many ways. We have two eyes that see the seven colors of the rainbow...

two ears that hear the sounds of
thunder and pitter-patter of the
raindrops on an umbrella...

and one nose that can smell the
sweetness of the roses.

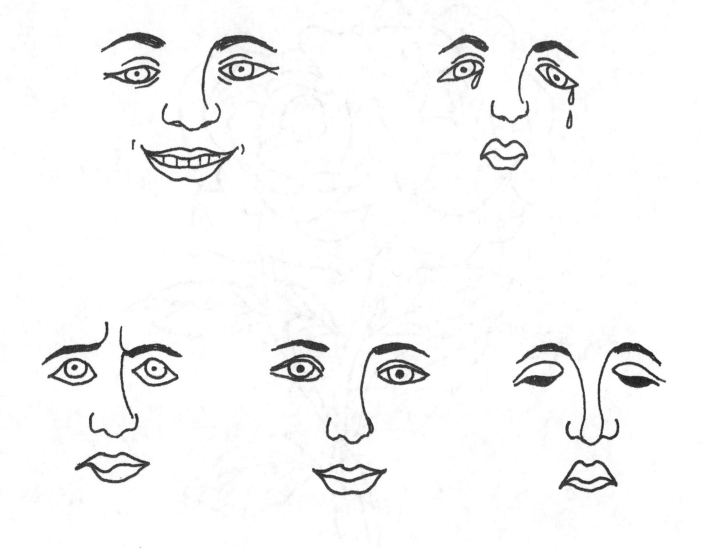

We all experience the same feelings
of happiness, sadness, anger, pride and
shame. We may speak many different
languages at home, but...

we all smile in the same language.

I wish I could tell the children at the bus stop that I look different, but inside I am just like them. I wish they would not look at me in a strange way, because it hurts my feelings. I wish I didn't have to stand alone.

I wish I could tell them...

I think I will tell them ... tomorrow!
I hope they will understand me.

I told them, "My hair is down to my waist and I wash it a few times a week. I get tangles but Mama takes them out very gently.

I am glad I told them about myself.

Interesting Facts About The Sikhs...

❖ The word "Sikh" means a student or learner or seeker of knowledge.

❖ The founders of this religion were known as Gurus

❖ Guru means a spiritual teachers or the one who dispels darkness of ignorance.

❖ The Sikh religion started with Guru Nanak in the 15th century.

❖ Guru Nanak simplified the concept of religion as a way of life as opposed to some rituals.

❖ The Sikhs had ten human Gurus in succession.

❖ The Tenth Guru, Guru Gobind Singh was the last human guru. He gave the Sikhs their unique identity with long hair and turban. Their identity gave the Sikhs self-confidence and instilled fearlessness in them.

❖ The Sikhs value their hair as a gift of their tenth Guru and keep it with utmost respect. It is impolite to touch their hair without permission.

❖ Most of the girls and women braid their long hair or roll it up and tuck it in a bun on the back of their heads although some wear turbans too.

❖ The boys and men tuck their hair in a bun on top of their head. The turban, a symbol of royalty in India, adorns a Sikh man's head. Men ought not trim their beards either.

❖ The Sikhs are easily recognized by their turbans, but their identity is still not understood by many. This ignorance results in severe harassment, teasing, bullying and sometimes beating of Sikh children in schools and prejudice and violence against Sikh men in public places.

❖ As the Sikh boys are ostracized by their peers because of their long hair, many parents cut young boys' hair as soon as they face such problems. These children are then denied the identity given to them by their heritage.

❖ Number 5 is very special to the Sikhs:

  ▪ They are the fifth largest religious denomination in the world.
  ▪ They have 5 articles of faith - long uncut hair, a small comb, a steel bracelet, a small sword and special boxer shorts. The names of these articles begin with the sound /k/ in Punjabi, the language of the Sikhs.
  ▪ The Sikhs originated in the state of Punjab. Punjab means the land of five rivers.
  ▪ There are 500,000 Sikhs in the United States of America.

It is the sincere hope of the author, that this book will help develop deeper understanding of the concerns of Sikh children so that they can follow their tradition with pride and be treated in a friendly manner by their peers. Teachers have huge power to transform lives of children. Please read The Boy With Long Hair to your students. Discuss the implication of bullying and teasing. You may use the Teaching Guidelines to teach literacy skill to your class. Share this powerful resource with your colleagues.

This book has been endorsed by the California Teachers' Association and listed by California Department of Education as a Supplementary Instructional Material (SIM). If you need to order more copies of this book, please visit www.Sikhfoundation.org.

Talking Points...

❖ **Which country did the Sikhs come from?**
(They originated in the state of Punjab in India).

❖ **Why do most of the Sikhs wear a turban or a patka?**
(The Sikhs men wear a turban and the boys wear a patka to keep their hair covered because they don't cut their hair.)

❖ **Why are the Sikh boys teased in schools?**
(Many people do not know the Sikh tradition of keeping uncut hair on their heads. This lack of knowledge results in severe harassment, teasing and sometimes beating of Sikh children in schools and prejudice and violence against Sikh men in public places.)

❖ **Why do some Sikh boys cut their hair?**
(As the Sikh boys are ostracized by their peers because of their long hair, many parents cut young boys' hair as soon as they face such problems. These children are then denied the identity given to them by their heritage.)

❖ **How many Sikhs live in the United States of America?**
(There are 500,000 Sikhs in the United States of America.)

Discussion Points

Personal stories of exclusion can make an interesting collection to publish and share. Here are some prompts that might start children off to writing.

1. Have you ever felt left out from a group? What was the reason? How did you feel? Who helped to make you feel better?

2. Have you ever excluded someone from your group? What was the reason? How did you feel? How do you think the other person felt?

3. Have you ever seen a group of children teasing another child just because he or she looked different to them? Describe the situation. What did you do about that? What could you have done at that time?

4. Why do you think children tease others? What can we do to stop children from teasing and harassing others?

5. Do you think this world would be a better place if no one teased and hurt anybody's feelings? Explain.

What is on their mind?

Imagine the scene below. What do you think these children are thinking?
Fill in the dialog bubbles.

TEACHING IDEAS

These activities are appropriate for second-third grade level and can be simplified for lower grades.

The Boy With Long Hair by Pushpinder Singh is intended to increase awareness of Sikh identity in our schools. Although this book focuses on one ethnic group, the Sikhs from India, the concept is of universal significance. Every day, many children are excluded from play groups at school, beaten up, humiliated and bullied because they look different. The Sikh boys are especially vulnerable as they have long, uncut hair that is tied in a bun on the top of their head. Below are some suggested activities you can follow after you have read the book The Boy With Long Hair to help young children develop empathy and understanding for the feelings of others.

LANGUAGE ARTS

☐ Ask the students to think about a person they don't get along with. They make a list of the ways in which they are different, and another list of the ways in which they are the same. Which list is longer? Are they surprised at the conclusion? Why or why not?

☐ Vocabulary: happiness, sadness, pride, anger, shame, and strange. To learn the spelling and meaning of the above words ask the students to:
  1. Look up the word meanings in dictionary.
  2. Write synonyms/antonyms for each word.
  3. Use each word in a sentence.

ORAL LANGUAGE

☐ This book lends itself to carry on a meaningful discussion in being sensitive, caring and compassionate towards each other.

WRITING AND PUBLISHING

Students of all ages love to see their work published. Their writing can be typed and bound as a class book. If possible, make multiple copies of the book and give one to each student. They would love to share and read them again and again.

☐ Personal stories of exclusion can make interesting collection to publish and share.

Here are some prompts that might start children off to writing.

1. Have you ever felt left out from a group? What was the reason? How did you feel? Who helped to make you feel better?

2. Have you ever excluded someone from your group? What was the reason? How did you feel? How do you think the other person felt?

3. Have you ever seen a group of children teasing another child just because he or she looks different? Describe the situation. What did you do about that? What could you have done?

4. Why do you think children tease others? What can we do to stop children from teasing and harassing others?

5. Do you think this world would be a better place if no one teased and hurt anybody? Why or why not? Draw a picture of a world where everyone fits in.

☐ There are number of writers' crafts in this book. You can teach the use of repetition, the ellipsis, use of and..., the short, short, long sentences to say a simple idea in a more creative way, thought bubbles, complete change in mood from beginning to the end etc.

MATH

☐ Make a bar graph, or a picture graph to represent the diverse ethnic groups in your classroom.

DRAMA

☐ Write a script about a time when you saw someone being teased. What did you do? What did you do to stop teasing? Do a role play in class or make video and post it on YouTube.

ART

☐ Illustrate the feeling words from the Language Arts section.

"It [*The Boy With Long Hair*] will do so much to make sure that hate crimes will not occur."
Assemblywoman Judy Chu

"The book is meant to educate children about cultural diversity and help promote an understanding and acceptance of our differences."
California Ex-Lt. Governor Cruz M. Bustamante

The Boy With Long Hair sparks our awareness of Sikh culture and makes accessible, to young and old alike, a taste of their rich heritage."
Mary Melnick, 5ᵗʰ Grade Teacher

"It all started when a boy with long hair came to our kindergarten class. He was called a girl and I didn't know what to say. Then I read *The Boy With Long Hair* and it all made sense... Children haven't teased him since or asked him anymore questions. They just understood and accepted him."
Donna Courtney, Kindergarten Teacher

This story touched my students and I deeply... We used it to make judgments, feel empathy and to be proud of who we are.
Florence Thisquin, 3ʳᵈ Grade Teacher

"When we read *The Boy With Long Hair* and discuss the character's experiences, we open our students to the uniqueness and differences in each culture."
Nathan Pham, Elementary School Teacher

"Every September I read *The Boy With Long Hair* to my second graders while working on our friendship unit. We celebrate the diversity in our school."
Thea Roseland, 2ⁿᵈ Grade Teacher

"An extremely important subject told in a very simple story!"
Kerry Brown, Editor

"This book made such a big difference in my child's life."
Pawan, mother of a Sikh boy

"This is my favorite book."
Kim Khanh N., a fourth grade student